**SADDLEBACK**
EDUCATIONAL PUBLISHING

**think green**

# Global Warming

**SADDLEBACK**
**EDUCATIONAL PUBLISHING**
Three Watson
Irvine, CA 92618-2767
Website: www.sdlback.com

ISBN-13: 978-1-59905-349-3
ISBN-10: 1-59905-349-7
eBook: 978-1-60291-677-7

Printed in China

12 11 10 09 08   9 8 7 6 5 4 3 2 1

# Contents

# Global Warming: An Introduction

Earth gets most of its heat from the sun. The sun's energy travels through space and enters Earth's atmosphere. Some of this energy is reflected back into space by the atmosphere and clouds, and some of it is absorbed and stored as heat by Earth's surface. When the surface and atmosphere become warm, they radiate heat back into space. This helps keep Earth from becoming too hot or too cold.

## What is global warming?

Global warming is the increase in average temperature of Earth's surface. Earth has warmed by about 1° F over the past 100 years. Our planet could be getting warmer on its own, but many scientists think it has happened because of human activities. A warmer Earth means frequent heat waves, rising sea levels, floods, droughts, wildfires, and epidemics.

## Causes of Global Warming

### Human Activities

The atmosphere contains gases that trap the sun's energy and keep Earth warm. These gases are called greenhouse gases. If the level of greenhouse gases in the atmosphere increases, more heat will be trapped, making Earth warmer. Burning of coal, oil, and natural gas emits large amounts of greenhouse gases into the atmosphere. Deforestation and various agricultural and industrial practices also contribute to an increase in greenhouse gases. This has led to an increase in the atmospheric temperature of Earth.

### Volcanic Eruptions

Volcanoes also release large amounts of water and carbon dioxide. Over long periods of time (thousands or millions of years), multiple eruptions of volcanoes can raise carbon dioxide levels enough to cause significant global warming.

### Solar Variations

The sun is the main source of energy for Earth's climate system. Small changes in the sun's energy over an extended period can lead to climate changes. Some scientists suspect that a portion of the global warming in the first half of the 20th century was due to an increase in the output of solar energy.

# Effects of Global Warming

### Scarcity of Water

Change in rainfall patterns is an important effect of global warming. Decreasing rainfall in many places has reduced groundwater. The water in coastal areas has become polluted by rising sea levels. These factors have contributed to severe shortages of drinking and irrigation water. It is estimated that by 2080 more than three billion people could suffer from water shortage. Northern Africa, the Middle East, and the Indian subcontinent will be the worst affected.

### Failing Crops

Long stretches of dry seasons caused by reduced rainfall have resulted in crop failures. Cereal crop yields are expected to drop significantly in Africa, the Middle East, and India.

### Changing Weather Patterns

Global warming has led to inevitable climate changes. Changing weather patterns have upset physical and biological systems in many parts of the world. Humans, animals, and plants alike have been affected by these changed weather patterns.

### Melting Sea Ice

Arctic sea ice continues to decline because of global warming. The current rate of decline is about 8% per decade. This means that by 2060 there will be no Arctic sea ice.

### Effect on Animals

The population of many species of polar animals has been reduced over the years. According to a survey, the polar bear population in Canada's western Hudson Bay has dropped by 22% since the late 1980s. Global warming has also shortened the polar bears' hunting season. This has reduced their body mass and led to reduced fertility. Female polar bears now give birth to fewer cubs. Studies have shown striking changes in other marine animals, too. The North Sea codfish has gotten smaller in size, and their reproductive abilities have become weak, too.

### Human Deaths

According to the World Health Organization (WHO), five million people fall ill and 150,000 die every year because of climate-related changes. WHO estimates that this figure could double by 2030.

### Did you know?

Current computer models have projected the Earth's average surface temperature could rise as much as 4° F to 11° F by the end of the 21st century.

# Earth Is Getting Hotter

Earth is getting hotter by about 0.36° F every 10 years. Some scientists believe this is because the sun is burning more brightly. Other scientists have shown that the increased emission of greenhouse gases and other chemicals such as methane, nitrous oxide, and halocarbons is responsible for making Earth hotter. The last 25 years were the warmest for the United States. In Europe, during the summer of 2003, thousands of people died due to extreme temperatures. Nearly 15,000 people died in France alone. Scientists believe that Earth will continue to get hotter and endanger human and animal lives.

## Diseases

Increasing temperatures have led to the outbreak of diseases such as malaria and dengue fever in areas that were previously unexposed to these diseases. Warmer temperatures extend the habitable zone for disease-carrying animals such as insects, rodents, and snails. Mosquitoes are particularly sensitive to temperature. They do not breed below 60.8 degrees Fahrenheit. However, climate shifts allow them to survive in formerly inhospitable areas at higher latitudes and altitudes. For example, in South America, the dengue fever virus previously could only be found at elevations of about 3,000 feet or lower, but now it can be found above 6,000 feet.

## Rising Sea Level

Warmer temperatures have led to the melting of glaciers and ice shelves, causing ocean water to expand. Most mountain glaciers have been melting over the past 150 years, and most will be gone by the year 2100. Global sea levels have risen by about 4 to 10 inches over the past 100 years, and an increase of another 6 to 33 inches is expected in the next hundred years. In the last 30 years, more than a million square miles of sea ice has disappeared.

### Did you know?

The temperature of Earth is expected to increase by 4° F to 11° F by 2100 if we do not reduce greenhouse gas emissions.

## Extreme Weather

Precipitation has increased worldwide. Heavy downpours and snowstorms in mid to high latitudes have led to severe floods, soil erosion, landslides, and damage to life and property. Increased temperatures have also intensified the drying out of soils in summer. Droughts have become widespread, and the risk of wildfires has become very high. In 2007, there were more than 85,000 wildfires in the United States, and more than 9.3 million acres were burned.

## Bleaching Reefs

Coral reefs are one of the most diverse and productive kinds of ecosystems in the world. Our planet's coral reefs are experiencing bleaching caused by the loss of algae on which corals survive. Corals bleach when the surface algae that covers them dies out, causing the corals to appear white. The warming of seawater is one of the reasons for coral bleaching.

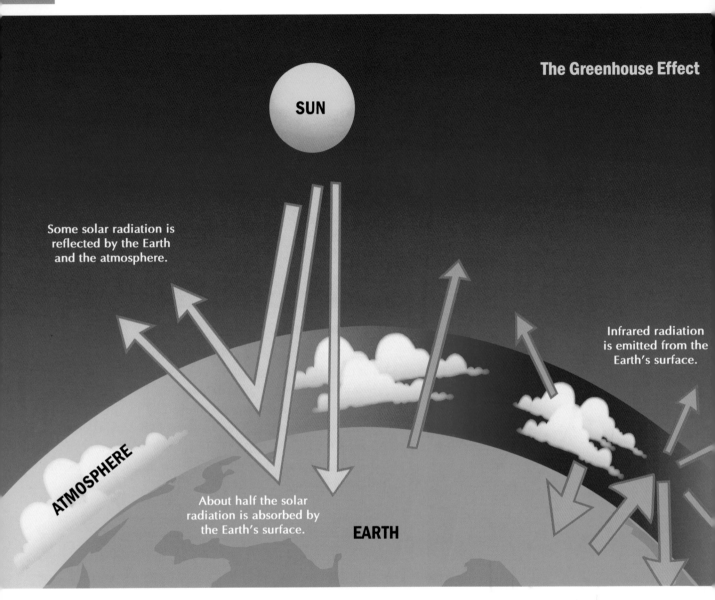

The Greenhouse Effect

SUN

Some solar radiation is reflected by the Earth and the atmosphere.

Infrared radiation is emitted from the Earth's surface.

ATMOSPHERE

About half the solar radiation is absorbed by the Earth's surface.

EARTH

# The Greenhouse Effect

Earth is surrounded by a layer of gases known as the *atmosphere*. Some of these gases, such as carbon dioxide, methane, and ozone, behave like glass in a greenhouse. These gases let the sun's energy pass through but prevent some of the heat from leaving Earth's atmosphere. Without these gases, Earth's temperature would be too cold for most life to exist. These gases are called *greenhouse gases*, and the phenomenon is called *the greenhouse effect*.

## Greenhouse Effect Sustains Life

The greenhouse effect helps to sustain life on Earth. Sufficient warmth and light are essential for any living organism. The greenhouse effect has warmed our planet for millions of years. Without the greenhouse effect, Earth would have been a much cooler place, with an average temperature of 0.4° F instead of its present 59° F. Humans, animals, and plants could hardly survive in such severe conditions. The greenhouse effect helps in creating a constant average temperature on Earth's surface.

## Enhanced Greenhouse Effect

The *enhanced greenhouse effect* is the increase in the natural greenhouse effect caused by manmade activities. It occurs at a much faster rate than the natural greenhouse effect. The enhanced greenhouse effect traps extra heat in the atmosphere, and that ultimately increases Earth's surface temperature. The enhanced greenhouse effect is an outcome of human activities such as the burning of fossil fuels such as oil, coal, and natural gas and the clearing of forests. Extensive agriculture, especially rice cultivation, produces methane. And the application of fertilizers and burning of biomass produce nitrous oxide, which is a potent greenhouse gas.

### Did you know?

The greenhouse effect is stronger on some planets and weaker on others. On Venus, for example, the greenhouse effect is so strong that the surface temperature can reach 900° F.

## Impacts of Enhanced Greenhouse Effect

The enhanced greenhouse effect is largely responsible for global warming. Some of the changes caused by the enhanced greenhouse effect:

- Climate change
- Melting of glaciers and rising of sea levels
- Submerging of many islands and coastal areas
- More rainfall and floods in certain areas
- Severe droughts leading to hunger and death
- Extinction of many species of plants and animals

### The Glass Greenhouse

A greenhouse is an enclosed building made of glass in which plants are grown. Greenhouses can be found in places where temperatures are too cold for plants to grow naturally. The glass in a greenhouse lets in light energy from the sun, which warms the air inside the greenhouse. The warm air inside cannot escape through glass. This keeps the greenhouse warm and protects the plants from the cold outside. Earth's atmosphere also behaves like the walls in a greenhouse. It lets in sunlight but traps heat and prevents it from returning to space.

# Greenhouse Gases

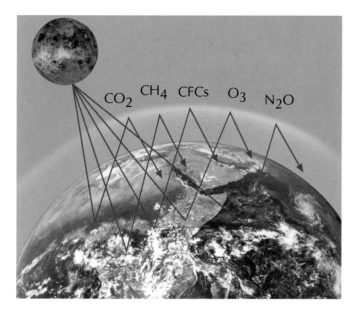

Greenhouse gases are atmospheric gases that trap solar radiation. Greenhouse gases create a natural warm cover for Earth. Some greenhouse gases are primarily natural gases and have always been there in the atmosphere. Others, like chlorofluorocarbons, are manmade and are rarely found in nature. The six major greenhouse gases are water vapor, carbon dioxide ($CO_2$), methane ($CH_4$), nitrous oxide ($N_2O$), ozone ($O_3$), and chlorofluorocarbons.

## Discovering Greenhouse Gases

French mathematician Jean Baptiste Fourier was the first scientist to suggest that the greenhouse effect existed. In 1827, Fourier noted that greenhouse gases kept Earth warm. About 30 years later, British physicist John Tyndall discovered that certain atmospheric gases could absorb and radiate heat. Tyndall showed that water vapor, carbon dioxide, and ozone were the best absorbers of solar radiation. In the 1890s, Swedish scientist Svante Arrhenius and an American, P. C. Chamberlain, independently studied carbon dioxide as a warming gas. They suggested that the burning of fossil fuels could cause Earth's temperature to change.

## Water Vapor

Water vapor is water in gaseous form. It is the most abundant greenhouse gas in the atmosphere. Water vapor accounts for about 60% to 70% of the natural greenhouse effect. With the increase in atmospheric temperature, more water is evaporated from lakes, rivers, and oceans. Warm air in the atmosphere can hold more water vapor. Higher amounts of water vapor absorb more heat radiated from Earth and contribute to global warming.

## Carbon Dioxide

Carbon dioxide is an important greenhouse gas. It is the most prominent contributor to the enhanced greenhouse effect and is responsible for 50% to 60% of the global warming from greenhouse gases produced by human activities. Carbon dioxide enters the atmosphere naturally through the carbon cycle. Human activities have produced more carbon dioxide in recent years. Carbon dioxide is released into the atmosphere by the burning of fossil fuels such as petroleum, natural gas, and coal. The amount of carbon dioxide in the atmosphere has increased by about 35% since the Industrial Revolution in the 1700s. The United States alone produces about 25% of the global carbon dioxide emissions.

## Methane

Methane is a natural greenhouse gas. The concentration of methane in the atmosphere is less than carbon dioxide; however, it is 21 times more effective in trapping heat than carbon dioxide. Methane is emitted into the atmosphere by both natural and human activities. It is released by landfills, swamplands, rice production, raising cattle, natural gas, and mining coal. Methane is the most rapidly increasing greenhouse gas. Methane emission has increased by about 145% since the Industrial Revolution. Methane accounts for about 20% of the overall global warming.

## Nitrous Oxide

Nitrous oxide, commonly known as "laughing gas," is one of the three major greenhouse gases. It can effectively trap about 300 times more heat than carbon dioxide. Excessive use of nitrogen-containing fertilizers, combustion of fossil fuels, and production of nitric acid can release nitrous oxide into the atmosphere. Every year human activities release 7 to 13 million tons of nitrous oxide into the air.

## Tropospheric Ozone

Ozone is a natural gas found in both the stratosphere and the troposphere. Ozone in the stratosphere shields us from the harmful ultraviolet rays of the sun, but ozone in the troposphere acts as a greenhouse gas. This ozone in the troposphere is often called "bad" ozone. Tropospheric ozone also contributes to smog, which can cause health problems. Unlike other greenhouse gases, ozone is not found throughout the atmosphere. It is limited to the air above cities and industrial areas. Ozone in the troposphere has increased by about 30% since the Industrial Revolution.

## Chlorofluorocarbons

Chlorofluorocarbons are major greenhouse gases. These synthetic gases are composed of carbon, chlorine, and fluorine. They are used in aerosol cans, refrigerants, air conditioners, aerosol propellants, and cleaning solvents. Chlorofluorocarbons react with stratospheric ozone molecules and destroy them. The use of chlorofluorocarbons, however, has been reduced greatly to protect the ozone layer.

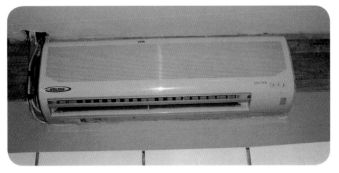

## How can we reduce greenhouse gas emissions?

- Plant more trees. Save forests. Stop deforestation.
- Use air conditioners only when required.
- Turn off lights and other energy-consuming devices when not in use.
- Use fluorescent light bulbs. Replacing one incandescent light bulb with fluorescent will save 150 pounds of carbon dioxide in a year.
- Use alternative fuels to run your vehicles.
- Reduce wastes and buy recyclable products.

## Did you know?

Carbon dioxide can remain in the atmosphere for 50 to 200 years.

# Ozone Layer Depletion

The sun provides us with light and heat, but its energy also contains ultraviolet radiation, which is harmful to humans and other living organisms. A layer of gases in the upper atmosphere absorbs most of these harmful ultraviolet rays from the sun. This protective layer of gases is called the ozone layer. The ozone layer is made up of ozone, which is a form of oxygen. This layer begins about six miles above Earth's surface and extends to about 30 miles. However, the ozone layer is being depleted in many places. Some greenhouse gases, such as chlorofluorocarbons, are destroying the ozone layer. As a result, harmful radiation from the sun is able to reach Earth.

## What does the ozone layer do?

The ozone layer filters harmful radiation from the sun. It prevents ultraviolet radiation from reaching Earth's surface. Ultraviolet radiation can cause skin cancer, cataracts, and snow blindness, and can affect some crops and aquatic life. The ozone layer absorbs 97% to 99% of the ultraviolet light radiated by the sun. This warms the atmosphere and helps to balance the temperature of Earth. It also protects humans, animals, and plants from the harmful effects of ultraviolet radiation. A 1% decrease in the ozone layer increases the amount of ultraviolet radiation exposure to Earth by 2%.

## Ozone-Destroying Chemicals

Chlorofluorocarbons are manmade chemicals that destroy the ozone in the atmosphere. Chlorofluorocarbons are stable, nonflammable chemicals that have been widely used in the last century in refrigeration, air conditioning, foams, aerosols, fire protection, and solvents. Once released, they rise upward for six to eight years before reaching the stratosphere. Chlorofluorocarbons in the stratosphere can survive for as long as 100 years. During this period, they are broken down into hydrogen, fluorine, and chorine by the sun's radiation. Each broken down chlorine atom can destroy tens of thousands of ozone molecules in the atmosphere. Other chemicals harmful to the ozone layer include nitrogen oxides (emitted from motor vehicles), methyl bromide (used as a pesticide), halons (used in fire extinguishers), and methyl chloroform (used as a solvent in industrial processes).

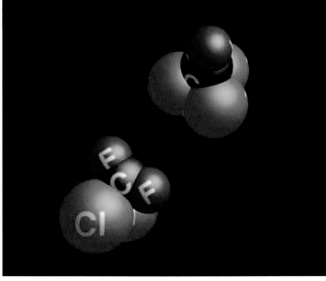

**CFCs Molecules**

## Ozone Hole

Every year a large "hole" forms in the ozone layer over the Antarctic region. The hole is actually a thinning of the ozone layer by almost 50%. The ozone hole over the Antarctic forms in late September for a period of our to six weeks. The ozone hole was discovered in 1985 by three British scientists, Joseph Farman, Brian Gardiner, and Jonathan Shanklin.

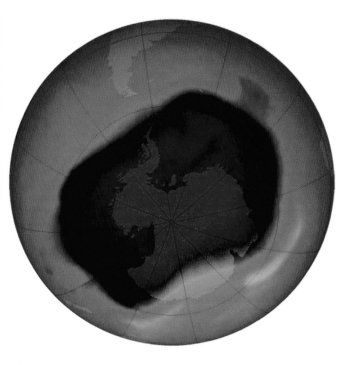

## Dobson Unit

The Dobson Unit (DU) is the unit for measuring ozone in the atmosphere. One Dobson Unit is almost 27 million ozone molecules per square centimeter. The average amount of ozone in the ozone layer is about 300 DU. An ozone hole will form if this concentration goes below 220 DU.

## The Montreal Protocol

The industrialized nations of the world have considered ozone layer depletion with much seriousness. Many discussions were held to limit production and consumption of ozone-damaging chemicals. The most important of these discussions was held in 1987 in Montreal, Canada. The industrialized nations created an agreement to reduce the production and consumption of chlorofluorocarbons. The agreement came to be known as The Montreal Protocol.

### How can we reduce ozone layer depletion?

- Use energy-efficient appliances.
- Use your electrical appliances wisely.
- Use less hot water.
- Choose a less polluting car.
- Use unleaded gas or alternative fuels.
- Insulate your house to keep it warmer in winter and cooler in summer.
- Buy air conditioners or refrigerators that do not use chlorofluorocarbons.
- Do not buy halon-based fire extinguishers.

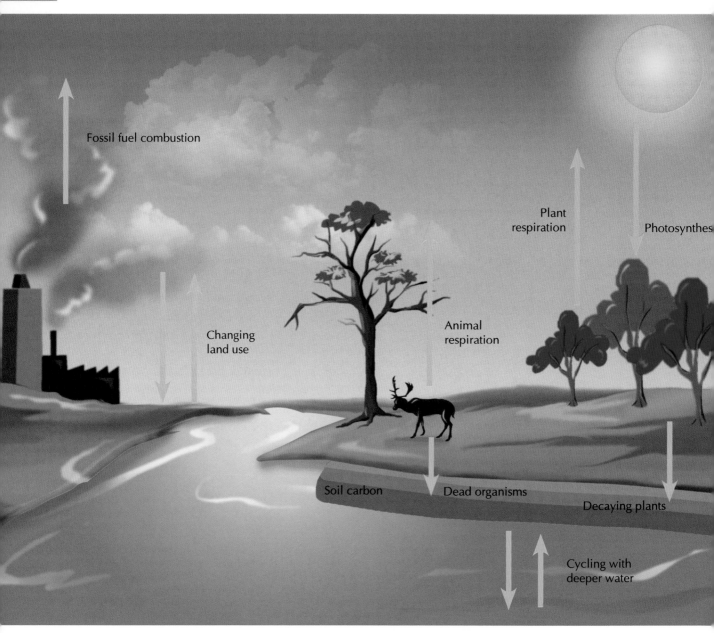

Fossil fuel combustion

Plant
respiration

Photosynthes

Changing
land use

Animal
respiration

Soil carbon

Dead organisms

Decaying plants

Cycling with
deeper water

# The Carbon Cycle

Carbon is an element found almost everywhere on Earth. It is found in living as well as nonliving matter. Carbon is stored in soil, forests, and oceans. Fossil fuels such as coal, oil, and natural gases are made up of carbon. Carbon moves from living and nonliving matter in different forms through land, water, and air. This movement of carbon is known as the *carbon cycle*.

## Carbon Exchange

- Carbon exists as carbon dioxide in the atmosphere. It enters the living world through plants and algae. Plants absorb carbon dioxide from the atmosphere and use the carbon atoms to manufacture food through photosynthesis and release oxygen into the atmosphere.
- Herbivorous animals eat plants and convert the carbon into food. Carnivores and omnivores eat these herbivorous animals and use the carbon present for metabolism.
- Carbon present in living plants and animals is returned back to Earth when these organisms die and their bodies decompose.
- Exchange of carbon dioxide also takes place between the oceans and the atmosphere. Marine plants absorb dissolved carbon dioxide in the water to produce their food.
- Fossil fuel burning by industry and automobiles are other processes of releasing carbon dioxide into the atmosphere.

## Carbon Dioxide Cycle

The carbon dioxide cycle is a process through which carbon dioxide is recycled in the environment. Carbon dioxide is a colorless and odorless greenhouse gas. It plays an important part in all plant and animal processes. Organisms that can photosynthesize absorb carbon dioxide and produce carbon-based products using water. Plants release oxygen during photosynthesis as a byproduct, and this oxygen is inhaled by animals during respiration. The respiration process is the reverse of photosynthesis.

### Where is carbon found in our planet?

**Carbon is found:**
- in living and dead organisms
- as organic matter in soil
- in gaseous form as carbon dioxide in the atmosphere
- in sedimentary rock deposits such as limestone
- as dissolved atmospheric carbon dioxide in the oceans
- as calcium carbonate shells in marine organisms

### Did you know?

The amount of carbon dioxide in our atmosphere decreases during the warmer season, as the rate of photosynthesis is high.

## Natural Carbon Dioxide Release

Carbon dioxide is released and removed from the atmosphere by the following natural processes:
- Animal and plant respiration
- Plant photosynthesis
- Ocean-atmosphere exchange, in which oceans absorb and release carbon dioxide at the sea surface
- Volcanic eruptions, during which carbon is released from rocks deep in Earth's crust

## Carbon Dioxide Emissions

Various human activities emit carbon dioxide into the atmosphere. About 22% of the current atmospheric carbon dioxide concentrations exist due to human activities. Production of mineral products such as lime and cement as well as production of various chemicals and metals adds to the amount of carbon dioxide in the atmosphere. Combustion of fossil fuels causes 70% to 75% carbon dioxide emissions. Deforestation and automobiles add up to 25% of carbon dioxide in the atmosphere.

# The Kyoto Protocol

The continuous and alarming increase of greenhouse gases is causing global warming. Most of these greenhouse gases are emitted by industrialized nations. In 1997, more than 160 nations agreed to reduce their collective emission of greenhouse gases. These nations met in the ancient Japanese capital of Kyoto and created an agreement that came to be known as the Kyoto Protocol.

## Ratifying the Kyoto Protocol

The Kyoto Protocol was signed by more than 140 countries. These countries promised to cut the amount of greenhouse gases they produced each year. They made many new rules and laws to reduce the amount of greenhouse gas emissions. The protocol came into effect on February 16, 2005, when it was ratified by Russia. This was important, because the protocol could become valid only if ratified by nations accounting for at least 55% of greenhouse gas emissions. The United States has since withdrawn from the Kyoto Protocol.

## The Agreements in the Kyoto Protocol

The Kyoto Protocol commits 38 industrialized countries to limit their greenhouse gas emissions. The objectives of the protocol are as follows:

- Individual targets have been set for each country based on its pollution levels.
- Targets have been set for a five-year period from 2008 through 2012.
- Targets are calculated as an average over five years.
- Cuts in carbon dioxide, methane, and nitrous oxide are to be measured against a base year of 1990.
- Cuts in long-lived industrial gases such as hydrofluorocarbons, perfluorocarbons, and sulfur hexafluoride will be measured against a 1990 or 1995 baseline.
- Growing, developing countries such as China and India are outside the framework.

## Percentage of Greenhouse Gas Reduction

- Switzerland and the European Union by 8%
- The Central and East European countries (Bulgaria, Czech Republic, Estonia, Latvia, Liechtenstein, Lithuania, Monaco, Romania, Slovakia, and Slovenia) by 8%
- The United States by 7%
- Canada, Hungary, Japan, and Poland by 6%

## Countries That Can Increase Emissions

- Iceland by 10%
- Australia by 8%
- Norway by 1%

### Did you know?

Japan is Asia's third largest carbon dioxide emitter. It is also the fifth biggest polluter in the world.

# Climate Change

Climate is the average weather conditions in a region or area over a period of several years. Different places have different climates. Climate change is the variation or change in the climate of a place. It includes changes in temperature and precipitation. Climate change may occur due to external forces, natural internal processes, or changes in the atmospheric composition. Climate change is taking place around the planet. It has resulted in the rise of sea levels, melting of glaciers, more severe floods, and worse storms.

## Causes of Climate Change

### Continental Drift

Around 200 million years ago, all the continents were joined together as a giant landmass or supercontinent. Gradually this giant landmass began to drift apart. Over many millions of years, it formed Earth's continents. This continental drift changed the physical features and position of landmasses. It also changed the position of water bodies. Continental drift changed the wind and ocean currents, thus affecting the climate of all places on Earth.

### Volcanoes

Volcanoes erupt and release large amounts of water vapor, sulfur dioxide, dust, and ash into the atmosphere. The large volumes of sulfur dioxide and dust reach the upper levels of the atmosphere and partially block the sun's rays, which results in cooling. The sulfur dioxide also combines with water to form tiny droplets of sulfuric acid. This reflects sunlight and screens the ground from some of the energy that it would ordinarily receive from the sun.

### Earth's Tilt

Changes in Earth's tilt affect the severity of the seasons. Greater tilt results in hotter summers and colder winters. Less tilt means cooler summers and warmer winters.

### Ocean Currents

Ocean currents absorb the sun's rays and move large amounts of heat across Earth. Heat escapes from the oceans in the form of water vapor, which is the most abundant greenhouse gas. Water vapor helps in the formation of clouds and has a cooling effect.

## Human Contribution to Climate Change

- Thermal power plants burn fossil fuels and emit greenhouse gases and pollutants.
- Private cars and public transportation run on gasoline and diesel, which are again fossil fuels.
- Large amounts of plastic waste generated by humans remain in the environment and cause damage.
- Increased use of paper and paper products leads to deforestation as more trees are cut.

### Did you know?

Rice is the world's most significant grain crop. Recent studies have shown that rice crops decrease by 10% for each degree of global warming.

## Effects of Climate Change

- Melting glaciers and the expansion of warmer seawater caused the approximately 4" to 10" rise in sea level during the 20th century. Scientists estimate that in the next 100 years, sea level may rise by as much as 33 inches. This will endanger the lives of people living near seacoasts as well as harming wetlands and coral reefs.
- Arctic sea ice is continuously melting and may cause changes in the world's ocean currents.
- Warming sea surface temperature affects marine life.
- Heavy rainfall causes flooding and other damage.
- Warming climates result in longer growing seasons in mid-latitude places and hot and dry tropical places.
- Higher temperatures cause high evaporation rates and extremely dry conditions.
- Warmer temperatures cause some animal species to migrate, which sometimes results in their dying. Polar animals and coral reefs are species endangered by global warming.
- Changes in temperature and rainfall affect agricultural yields.
- Human health is affected by increased heat stress.

## Ways to Decrease Adverse Climate Change

- Use renewable resources of energy such as solar energy, wind energy, alternative fuels, biomass energy, and hydroelectricity.
- Use energy efficiently.
- Prevent deforestation. Deforestation causes 17% of the release of atmospheric carbon dioxide.

# Severe Weather

Severe weather is a harsh phenomenon that is a threat to human life and property. It generally refers to severe thunderstorms, tornadoes, hurricanes, heat waves, snowstorms, floods, hail, and blizzards. Many scientists think global warming has led to an increase in severe weather conditions around the world. In recent years, many parts of the world have seen record high and low temperatures, extreme rainfall, and severe storms.

## Thunderstorms

*Thunderstorms* are a type of severe storm. They produce tornadoes, lightning, gusty winds, heavy rain, and hail. Global warming has led to an increase in the surface temperatures of seawater. The warmer water evaporates more quickly, causing thunderstorms to form more easily. Thunderstorms are often dangerous. In the United States, hundreds of people are injured and killed every year because of thunderstorms.

## Lifecycle of Thunderstorms

- Developing stage: Warm, moist air rises, creating a column of clouds. Occasional lightning occurs and lasts for about 10 minutes.
- Mature stage: The first rain, hail, strong winds, frequent lightning, and thunder occur. The storm appears black or dark green and lasts for 10 to 20 minutes or longer.
- Dissipating stage: Warm, moist air can no longer rise upward. The clouds begin to evaporate, and the intensity of the rain and wind decreases.

## Flash Floods

Flash floods need heavy rain to occur. When thunderstorms move slowly, flash floods can occur. Condensation of moist air produces large raindrops and causes heavy rain. More than eight inches of rain per hour can fall if the air is humid enough. Flash floods associated with thunderstorms cause hundreds of deaths every year.

## Tornadoes

*Tornadoes,* or *twisters,* are rotating, funnel-shaped columns of air that can occur at the end of the mature stage of a thunderstorm. They form at the bottom of a thundercloud and sometimes touch the ground. Tornadoes are rated for intensity according to a scale known as the F-scale, or Fujita scale. The scale was developed by Dr. Theodore Fujita in 1971. The F-scale or Fujita scale contains six categories, from F0 for weakest to F5 for the strongest tornadoes. The scale rates tornadoes according to wind speed and potential damage.

# Severe Weather Safety Rules

## Tornadoes

- When tornadoes occur, go to the lowest floor of the house, such as the basement or an interior room.
- Protect yourself from flying waste by wrapping blankets or overcoats around your body.
- Avoid areas such as auditoriums and warehouses.
- Do not stay in places that have exterior walls or glassy areas.
- Avoid sitting in cars and in mobile homes during tornadoes.
- Try to be in a designated tornado shelter.
- Cover your head with your hands and lie down flat in the nearest ditch or depression.

## Lightning

- Do not use telephones or other electrical appliances.
- Avoid taking a shower or bath.
- If you are in water, immediately get out and move to a safe area.
- If you are in a wooded area, move under a thick growth of small trees.
- Do not shelter under isolated trees or near water bodies, fences, tractors, or motorcycles.
- Do not lie flat on the ground.

## Flash Floods

- Avoid flood-prone areas while driving.
- Do not use low water crossings.
- If your vehicle stalls in floodwaters, get out immediately and leave it.
- Avoid flooded creeks, streams, and drainage ditches.
- Try to climb to higher ground.

# River Floods

## Before

- Keep a first aid kit ready.
- Try to know about your flood risk. You can also gather weather information from the Internet.
- Have enough fuel in your vehicle.
- Store as much drinking water as possible.
- Store some food products.

## Did you know?

Tornadoes in the northern hemisphere spin counterclockwise, while in the southern hemisphere they spin clockwise.

- Keep a radio handy during river floods.
- Keep emergency cooking equipment and a flashlight.

## During and After

- Avoid driving in flooded areas.
- Do not allow children to play near high water or storm drains.
- Drink boiled water.
- Do not eat food that has been exposed to flood waters.
- Avoid disaster areas.
- Make sure electrical equipment is dry before using it.
- Use flashlights instead of torches, lanterns, or matches inside a building.

| Original Fujita Scale | | Operational Fujita Scale (mph, 3-second gust) |
|---|---|---|
| F0 Gale Tornado 40-72 mph | Damage to chimneys and signboards. Broken tree branches and uprooted shallow-rooted trees. | 65-85 |
| F1 Moderate Tornado 73-112 mph | Hurricane-force winds begin in the lower limit. Surface of roofs peeled off. Mobile homes and automobiles pushed over. | 86-110 |
| F2 Significant Tornado 113-157 mph | Roofs torn off frame houses. Mobile homes demolished. Boxcars pushed over, large trees uprooted. Generates light-object missiles. | 111-135 |
| F3 Severe Tornado 158-206 mph | Severe damage. Roofs and walls torn off well-constructed homes. Overturned trains. Most forest trees uprooted. Heavy cars thrown. | 136-165 |
| F4 Devastating Tornado 207-260 mph | Well-constructed homes destroyed. Structures with weak foundations blown off. Cars thrown and large missiles generated. | 166-200 |
| F5 Incredible Tornado 261-318 mph | Phenomenal damage. Strong frame homes disintegrate or are lifted off foundations and carried considerable distance. | over 200 |

# Heat Waves

A heat wave is an abnormal rise in the temperature of an area, usually during the warm summer months. Temperatures during a heat wave rise above 90° F or more. Heat waves can last from a few days to several weeks.

## Are heat waves dangerous?

Although not as dangerous as other extreme weather events such as floods, tornadoes, and earthquakes, heat waves have been responsible for many deaths in the last few years. In the United States, 20,000 people were killed in heat waves between 1936 and 1975. The most disastrous heat wave of 1980 killed more than 1,250 people. In 1995, a heat wave killed over 1,000 people across the midwest and east coast.

## Heat-Related Health Problems

- Severe sunburn: Sunburn damages the skin, causes a reduction of the skin's ability to release excess heat, and makes the skin prone to heat-related problems.
- Heat cramps: Heat cramps, such as muscular pain and spasms in the abdomen and legs, are caused by overexertion, which leads to excess loss of water from the body through heavy perspiration.
- Heat exhaustion: Heat exhaustion leads to weakness, heavy sweating, clammy skin, a weak pulse, vomiting, and fainting.
- Heatstroke: Heatstroke is also known as sunstroke. The body's internal thermostat ceases to work during a heatstroke. Increased body temperature causes brain damage and even death if not treated immediately.

## Heat Index

Heat index gives a measure of how hot it actually feels outside. It also takes into account the amount of moisture in the air, which is added to the actual air temperature. Heat index rises by 15° F when exposed to full sunshine.

| Relationship Between Heat Index and Heat Disorder | |
|---|---|
| 130° F or higher | Heatstroke/sunstroke highly likely with continued exposure |
| 105-130° F | Sunstroke, heat cramps, or heat exhaustion likely with prolonged exposure |
| 90-105° F | Sunstroke, heat cramps, or heat exhaustion possible with prolonged exposure and/or physical activity |
| 80-90° F | Fatigue possible with prolonged exposure and/or physical activity |

## Heat Wave Precautions

- Drink plenty of water regularly, even when not feeling thirsty. Water keeps the body cool.
- Do not drink liquids with alcohol or caffeine. They affect the heart and dehydrate the body.
- Avoid high-protein foods. They increase metabolic heat.
- Avoid salt tablets.
- Eat regular small meals.
- Wear lightweight, light-colored clothes. Light colors reflect sunlight.
- Stay inside the house in air-conditioned rooms.
- Go to the lowest floor of the building if air conditioning is not available.
- Slow down and avoid strenuous activity.

### Did you know?

It is predicted that in the second half of the 21st century, heat waves in Europe and North America will become more common and more extreme.

## Where to Go During a Heat Wave

- Movie theater
- Local mall
- Restaurant
- Library
- Senior citizens' center

## How to Treat Heat Emergencies

- **Heat cramps:** Take the person to a cooler place. Let him or her rest. Lightly stretch the affected muscles. Replenish fluids; give the person half a glass of cool water every 15 minutes.
- **Heat exhaustion:** Take the person out of the heat to a cooler place. Remove tight clothes and provide wet, cool clothes. Give cool water to drink.
- **Heatstroke:** Take the person to a cooler place. Cool the person with a cool bath or wrap with wet sheets and fan him or her. Keep the person in a lying position. Do not give anything to drink or eat if the person refuses water or feels nauseated.

# Earlier Spring

Seasonal change is a climatic phenomenon. Temperature is an important part of climate. Every season occurs in a particular range of temperatures. Variation in temperatures of Earth's surface leads to changing of seasons. During the last 100 years, global warming has warmed Earth by about 1° F. During this time, the average minimum temperature of Earth has increased rapidly. This rapid increase of the minimum temperature has caused lengthening of the warm season. Spring marks the beginning of the warm season. In the northern hemisphere, spring is arriving about 1.2 days earlier every 10 years. Earlier spring affects the life cycle of plants and animals. This has a negative impact on the entire ecosystem.

## Earlier Spring and Thawing of Frozen Soil

The early arrival of spring in the last few years in high-latitude areas has led to the early thawing or melting of ice. For thousands of years, the frozen soil in the tundra and boreal forests of high-latitude areas has absorbed large amounts of carbon. Earlier warm temperatures cause early thawing of the frozen soil, which helps to release the stored carbon into the atmosphere. The released carbon reacts with oxygen in the air to make carbon dioxide. This increases the concentration of greenhouse gases in the atmosphere, which adds to global warming.

## Earlier Spring and Animal Adaptation

Spring is breeding time for many animals. Earlier spring has shortened the hibernation period of mammals and the egg-laying patterns of birds. Earlier spring also advances the breeding period. A study in Colorado shows that the hibernation of marmots is ending about three weeks earlier than it was 30 years ago. In the United States and Canada, the average egg-laying date for swallows has advanced by nine days since 40 years ago. The earlier arrival of spring will affect their population significantly.

## Earlier Spring and Bird Migration

Birds migrate in response to changes in weather, availability of food, and for breeding. In summer, they move to cooler places. Now with the early arrival of spring, birds are migrating earlier than usual. Scientists have found that the migratory birds of Australia are now arriving on an average of 3.5 days earlier per decade and leaving 5.1 days later.

### Did you know?

Over the last 15 years, loggerhead sea turtles off Florida's Atlantic coast are now laying eggs 10 days earlier.

## Earlier Spring and Blooming

Spring is also the blooming season. The warming of Earth's atmosphere and early arrival of spring is affecting plants as well as animals. Plants have now begun to bloom one or two days earlier every decade. In the United States, scientists have found that lilacs are blooming four days earlier. Apples and grapes are blooming six to eight days earlier as compared to 1965. Flowering plants like wild geraniums and columbines are also blooming earlier than before.

### What animals are being affected?

- Elephant seal pups' prey is migrating to cooler waters. This is making the elephant seal pups leaner.
- The breeding period of Canadian red squirrels is arriving 18 days earlier.
- Red foxes are moving north in search of cooler regions.
- The breeding period of North American Fowler's toads is arriving six days later than a decade ago.
- In search of cooler waters, many fish species are moving northward.

# Heavy Rain

Water evaporates and condenses to form liquid droplets, which form clouds in the atmosphere. Rain consists of water falling in drops from clouds. Rain is an important part of the water cycle on Earth. Too much rain, however, can cause a lot of damage. Scientists have found that global warming is causing heavy rain in many parts of the world. A warmer atmosphere contains more water vapor, which leads to higher rainfall.

## Heavy Rain in the Northern Hemisphere

Global warming is causing heavy rain across parts of the northern hemisphere. New studies by scientists have shown that this increase of heavy rain is due to emissions of greenhouse gases by humans. Climate change in Britain has seen extremely heavy rain during the summers.

## Water Can Be Dangerous

Despite its important role in the existence of life on Earth, water in the form of heavy rain can be dangerous. Heavy rain occurs when the precipitation rate is greater than .3 inches per hour. A monsoon is a seasonal wind or air mass caused by the effects of heating and brings rain. The largest monsoon is the Indian monsoon found in the Indian Ocean and southern Asia.

## Major Floods of Australia

| Year | Place | Cause | Destruction |
|---|---|---|---|
| 1893 | Brisbane, Queensland | Brisbane River banks broke | Washed away Albert Railway bridge at Indooroopilly. |
| 1954 | New South Wales | Heavy rain | Water flooded houses at great speed. |
| 1955 | Dubbo, Tamworth, Wellington, Narromine, and Warren | Heavy rain | Damaged fences, roads, railways, and bridges. Many farm animals killed. |
| 1973 | Northern Territory | Rivers and stagnant pools overflowed. | No destruction, but a good flow of water to arid desert. Therefore, it was a beneficial flood. |

## During Heavy Rain

- Avoid driving during heavy rain. About 80% of flood deaths occur in vehicles.
- Do not try to walk through water, streams, or rivers when they are in full flow. Just six inches of rapidly moving water can knock a person down.
- Vacate your home or office after turning off the utilities.

## After Heavy Rain

- Check for structural damage to houses and other buildings.
- Use a flashlight in darkness instead of candles, in case of gas leaks.
- Dispose of foods, including canned goods, which have been exposed to flood water.

### Did you know?

Each year, about 80 people are killed and nearly 300 are injured by lightning in the United States.

## Floods

Floods are caused by continuous heavy rain. Heavy rain pours excessive water into rivers and lakes. This overflow of water submerges land, causing floods. Flooding generally occurs in broad, flat lands situated on riverbanks or a main waterway.

## Before the Flood

- Shift important items to a higher level.
- Take outdoor items inside the house, as they may become damaged.
- Make sure to keep a supply of drinking water with you. Municipal water supplies can be contaminated by heavy rains.

# Heat Harms the Atmosphere

The *atmosphere* is the thin layer of gases that surrounds Earth. This layer protects our planet from the sun's harmful rays and helps support all life on Earth. The atmosphere is composed of nitrogen, oxygen, argon, carbon dioxide, water vapor, and traces of other gases. It is about 300 miles thick and is divided into several layers. The temperatures in these layers vary widely, from about 62° F to -135° F and can rise to more than 3,092° F in the outer atmosphere.

## Composition of the Atmosphere

The atmosphere is composed primarily of two gases, nitrogen and oxygen. These two gases make up 99% of the atmosphere. Nitrogen contributes about 78% and oxygen about 21%. The composition of other gases is about 0.9% argon and 0.03% carbon dioxide. The atmosphere also contains water vapor and minute quantities of other gases known as *trace gases.*

## Keeping the Earth Warm

Earth is kept warm by the atmosphere. The gases present in the atmosphere allow sunlight to pass through but prevent most solar energy from escaping into space.

When sunlight passes through the atmosphere, it strikes and warms Earth's surface. Sunlight striking Earth's surface gives off radiation that rises into the atmosphere. Most of this radiation is absorbed or prevented from escaping into space by carbon dioxide, water vapor, and other trace gases present in the atmosphere. This effect, also known as the natural greenhouse effect, keeps Earth warm.

## Greenhouse Gases

The gases that absorb or prevent radiation from escaping into space are known as *greenhouse gases*. They redirect radiation back to Earth's surface, where it is once again absorbed. Water vapor is the main greenhouse gas. Carbon dioxide, methane, nitrous oxide, and chlorofluorocarbons are other important greenhouse gases. The concentration of these gases in the atmosphere controls the amount of heat energy added to the atmosphere. The last century has seen a rapid increase in the concentration of these greenhouse gases. This has led to a rise in average global temperatures. The main reason for this massive increase in greenhouse gases is pollution from the burning of fossil fuels. Scientists predict that if the emission of greenhouse gases is not reduced it will lead to a further increase in global temperatures.

### Did you know?

The year 2005 was the warmest in the last 100 years. The other four warmest years over the last century were 1998, 2002, 2003, and 2004, respectively.

### Effects of Increasing Greenhouse Gases

The increased emission of greenhouse gases has led to global warming. If the current rate of emission of greenhouse gases continues, it could affect all life forms on Earth. Major effects of a rapid temperature rise:

- Very large changes in climate
- A rapid extinction of many species
- Melting of glaciers
- Rising sea levels
- Flooding of coastal areas
- Frequent extreme weather conditions
- Exposure to non-native diseases
- Change in the types of crops being grown in different parts of the world

# Heat Increases Hurricane Strength

Hurricanes are violent tropical storms. They originate in the oceans, near the tropics. Hurricanes are accompanied by heavy rainfall and winds blowing at speeds of 74 mph or more. Hurricanes cause a lot of property destruction and kill many people. Global warming does not *create* hurricanes, but it makes them stronger and more destructive. Some scientists believe warmer oceans make hurricanes stronger.

## Peak Season for Hurricanes

Hurricanes have specific seasonal patterns. The peak season for hurricanes in the northern hemisphere is June to November. In the southern hemisphere, most hurricanes develop from January to March.

## Global Warming Has Increased the Intensity of Hurricanes

Scientists believe that hurricanes have become more destructive over the past 30 years. Global warming could increase their intensity even more in the future. This is because global warming has led to a rise in the surface temperature of tropical ocean water. This rise has resulted in a 50% increase in the wind speeds and duration of hurricanes. This increased power of hurricanes has seen an upward trend in the destructive potential of hurricanes.

## Parts of a Hurricane

### Eye

The *eye* is the center of a hurricane, around which spiral bands of the storm rotate.
The eye does not have any clouds  but has some wind and rain. It is calm compared to the rest of the hurricane.

### Eye Wall

The *eye wall* is a circle of clouds that immediately surrounds the eye of the hurricane. It looks like a bright cloud ring right around the eye. It is the strongest area of the hurricane, where the fiercest winds and most intense rainfall occur.

### Spiral Bands

*Spiral bands* are clouds that surround the eye wall. They form the largest area of a hurricane. They produce rain and fierce winds. Most flooding occurs because of the rain from spiral bands.

## Stages of a Hurricane

1. **Tropical disturbance**: Hurricanes begin their life cycle as *tropical disturbances*. In this stage, thunderclouds start to group together in an organized cluster around a center of low pressure. Wind speeds are less than 25 miles per hour.
2. **Tropical depression**: A tropical disturbance becomes a *tropical depression* when the tropical winds begin to swirl in a cyclonic pattern because of the continuous drop in air pressure. Winds near the center are constantly between 23 and 39 miles per hour.
3. **Tropical storm**: A depression becomes a *tropical storm* with sustained wind speeds of 39–73 miles per hour. It is at this time that it is assigned a name. A tropical storm almost resembles a hurricane in appearance.
4. **Hurricane**: A tropical storm becomes a *hurricane* if the surface pressure continues to drop and winds reach 74 miles per hour. At this stage, the hurricane has a well-defined eye with spiral rain bands rotating around it.

## Hurricane Ratings

Hurricanes are rated according to a scale known as the Saffir-Simpson scale. This scale was developed by two American scientists, Herbert Saffir and Robert Simpson. The Saffir-Simpson scale contains five categories and rates hurricanes according to wind speed, storm surge, and the amount of damage that it could produce.

|  | Winds | Storm Surge | Potential Damage |
|---|---|---|---|
| Category 1 | 74–95 mph | 4 to 5 feet | Damage to unanchored mobile homes and trees. |
| Category 2 | 96–110 mph | 6 to 8 feet | Damage to trees, poorly constructed signs, and piers. Flooding of coastal and low-lying areas. |
| Category 3 | 111–130 mph | 9 to 12 feet | Serious damage to mobile and small homes. Large trees blown down. Floating debris damages larger structures. |
| Category 4 | 131–155 mph | 13 to 18 feet | Almost total damage to small homes. Complete destruction of some homes, especially mobile homes. Major coastal flooding damage. |
| Category 5 | above 155 mph | above 18 feet | Massive evacuation of residential areas on low ground. |

| Destructive Power Comparison | |
|---|---|
| Category 2 | 10 times more destructive than Category 1 |
| Category 3 | 50 times more destructive than Category 1 |
| Category 4 | 100 times more destructive than Category 1 |
| Category 5 | 250 times more destructive than Category 1 |

## Kinds of Damage Caused by Hurricanes

There are three main kinds of damage caused by hurricanes:

1. **Wind damage:** Hurricane winds can destroy small and mobile homes. Floating debris, such as signs, roofing material, siding, and small items left outside, becomes flying missiles in hurricanes.
2. **Storm surge damage:** The onshore rush of high ocean waves caused by a hurricane is known as a storm surge. The surge of high water that sweeps across the coastline poses the greatest threat to human life and property. Storm surges cause extensive flooding, which often accounts for the majority of the damage caused by hurricanes.
3. **Flood damage:** Inland areas face the major threat of widespread torrential rains, which can cause deadly and destructive floods.

# Arctic Ice Melting

The Arctic is a vast region near the North Pole. It is covered in ice and snow throughout the year. The Arctic region plays a major role in the global weather system and ocean circulation. The snow and ice form a protective, cooling layer and deflect solar radiation, which helps to maintain Earth's temperature. With the rise in average temperature, the Arctic ice caps are melting. In the last 50 years, the average temperature in the Arctic region has increased by 4° F to 7° F. Every 10 years the Arctic loses about another 9% of its ice. If we continue to emit greenhouse gases, the Arctic temperature may rise by 7° F to 13° F in the next 100 years

## Reasons for Arctic Ice Melting

Scientists have found two main reasons for Arctic ice melting: rising air temperatures and warmer seawaters. Rising air temperatures melt the ice from above, while warm seawater attacks it from below. Summers in the Arctic region are getting longer. During summer, the thinning of the ice cover can be as much as 40%.

## The Arctic Now

The Arctic region has seen dramatic changes in the last 100 years. It is a highly volatile region and is being affected by changing global climate. The ice cover has been greatly reduced and is now probably the smallest it's been in the last 100 years. This has happened because of the dramatic rise in the average temperatures in the region. The Arctic region has seen its temperature rise twice as fast as other regions of the world. The shrinking ice cover has affected the feeding and migration patterns of many Arctic animals, including polar bears, whales, walruses, and seals.

## Effects of Arctic Ice Melting

- Glaciers are shrinking and sea levels are rising around the world.
- Native people, plants, and wildlife have been affected by the melting of Arctic ice.
- Arctic ice melting can affect the traditional lifestyles of the region's people. It could also damage the infrastructure.
- The number of storms in coastal regions has increased, often resulting in land erosion.
- The Arctic ice melting has raised levels of ultraviolet radiation.
- The melting of ice has affected the marine food chain. It also means lack of habitat for animals like polar bears, seals, and other marine animals.
- Spruce bark beetles are famous for killing spruce trees. They breed faster in spring, and the Arctic region now has warmer weather. From 1993 to 2003, spruce bark beetles chewed up 3.4 million acres of Alaskan forest.
- Melting Arctic ice is responsible for unusual weather conditions.
- The Arctic vegetation regions are shifting, and ice and sea animals are losing their hunting space.
- Ringed seals are the primary food source of the Inuit people, but because of the reduction and destabilization of sea ice, the number of ringed seals is declining.

## Ward Hunt Ice Shelf Breakup

The Ward Hunt Ice Shelf is the Arctic's largest. It was originally part of a large ice shelf that broke up into a number of smaller shelves because of rising temperatures. It is located on the northern coast of Ellesmere Island in northern Canada. The ice shelf has been in place for about 3,000 years. In the summer of 2002, graduate student Derek Mueller discovered that the Ward Hunt Ice Shelf was breaking up. The shelf eventually broke in two. A massive freshwater lake that was dammed up behind the shelf spilled three billion cubic meters of fresh water into the Arctic Ocean. Scientists believe the breakup of the shelf was caused by the increase in the average temperature of the region. The temperature rise in the Arctic region is a result of global warming.

## Effects of Ward Hunt Ice Shelf Breakup

The breakup of ice shelves creates icebergs that float in the sea. These icebergs are a potential danger to ships moving in the region. They also affect offshore development, such as oil rigs. The release of fresh water may also have future ecological impacts.

## The Effects of Ice Shelf Decline

The loss of sea ice can have major implications for global climate. The decline of ice shelves may affect wildlife and human life. Sea ice reflects most of the sun's energy back into space. When the ice melts, it becomes seawater. This seawater absorbs most of the solar radiation rather than reflecting it. The melting of ice shelves means that more radiation will be absorbed by seawater, making Earth hotter, which contributes to global warming.

## Arctic Warming

Since the beginning of the 20th century, there has been a 41° F rise in air temperatures in the Arctic. This rise in air temperatures is due to global climate change. Over the last two decades there has been an eightfold increase in surface warming as compared to the previous 100 years. Several areas in the Arctic are warming by 2.5% each decade

### Did you know?

About 81% of Greenland is covered with ice, which contains enough water to raise the global sea level by about 21 feet.

# Worldwide Pollution

Pollution is any form of contamination of land, water, and air. Pollution is harmful to human health and causes damage to the environment. It usually is caused by human activities in some way. Every day harmful substances such as poisonous gases and chemicals are released into the air, polluting the environment. Pollution is broadly divided into four different types: air pollution, water pollution, land pollution, and noise pollution.

## Air Pollution

*Air pollution* is caused by chemicals in the air. Industries and vehicles that burn fossil fuels are two main sources of air pollutants. Other sources include natural radioactivity, volcanic eruptions, wind erosion, evaporation of organic compounds, and forest fires. About 90% of all air pollution in the United States is caused by burning of fossil fuels by power plants and automobiles.

## Water Pollution

Water can be polluted by agricultural, domestic, or industrial wastes. Sewage and fertilizers used in fields contain nitrates and phosphates that kindle the growth of aquatic plants and algae. Disproportionate growth of these organisms reduces the amount of oxygen in the water, thereby impairing the respiration of fish and other marine animals and plants. Sewage and fertilizers clog our waterways, too. The Mississippi River, which drains nearly 40% of the mainland of the United States, carries about 1.5 million metric tons of nitrogen pollutants into the Gulf of Mexico in a year.

## Land Pollution

Mismanagement of land resources causes *land pollution*. This causes erosion, degradation, and salinization of our soils. Harmful acids, pesticides, chemicals, radioactive waste, sewage sludge, and other types of hazardous waste that find their way to landfill sites are major threats to land. We lose around 15 million acres of prime agricultural land every year because of overuse and mismanagement.

## Causes of Land Pollution

- Agriculture
- Mining and quarrying
- Sewage sludge
- Dredged spoils
- Household wastes
- Demolition and construction
- Industrial wastes

## Noise Pollution

*Noise pollution* is a serious problem in most urban areas. Most modern towns andcitiesexperience a constant roar from vehicles, machines, and sirens. Noise can affect our hearing abilities and can cause other health problems, too.

## Sources of Noise Pollution

Major sources of noise pollution:
- Road traffic noise
- Air traffic
- Rail traffic
- Neighborhood and domestic noise
- Industrial noise

## Radioactive Pollution

Radioactive pollution is caused by nuclear reactions. Nuclear power plants, nuclear weapons, and transportation and disposal of nuclear waste cause radioactive pollution.

## What can you do to prevent pollution?

- Recycle as much waste as you can.
- Avoid using disposable items such as paper plates and plastic cups that become waste.
- Walk or use a bicycle whenever possible.
- Avoid processed food and drink.
- Buy organic food.
- Make compost of waste food.

### Did you know?

Nearly 40% of rivers and 46% of lakes in the United States are too polluted for swimming and fishing.

# Air Pollution

Air pollution is the contamination of our air. Various chemical, physical, and biological pollutants contaminate air. Air pollution is very dangerous, as these harmful pollutants often enter our bodies when we breathe. Inside our bodies, they can cause many serious diseases. Major sources of air pollution include factories, power plants, dry cleaners, cars, buses, trucks, and wildfires. One of every three Americans live in areas with unhealthy air.

## Major Air Pollutants

### Carbon Monoxide (CO)

*Carbon monoxide* is a colorless, odorless gas produced by the incomplete burning of carbon-based fuels including gasoline, diesel, and wood. It is also produced from the combustion of natural and synthetic products such as cigarettes.

### Carbon Dioxide ($CO_2$)

*Carbon dioxide* is the main greenhouse gas. It is produced by burning coal, oil, and natural gases.

### Chlorofluorocarbons (CFCs)

*Chlorofluorocarbons* are synthetic compounds containing carbon, chlorine, fluorine, and sometimes hydrogen. They are commonly used in air conditioners, refrigerators, cleaning solvents, and the manufacture of foams.

### Lead

Lead is present in gasoline, diesel, lead batteries, paints, hair dye products, etc.

### Ground Level Ozone

*Ground level ozone* is emitted by vehicles and industries.

### Nitrogen Oxides (NOx)

*Nitrogen oxides* are produced by burning fuels, including gasoline, diesel, and coal.

### Suspended Particulate Matter (SPM)

*SPM* consists of tiny airborne particles (or *aerosols*) that remain suspended in the air in the form of smoke, dust, and vapor.

### Respirable Particulate Matter (RSPM)

*RSPM* are tiny pollutant particles of liquids, hydrocarbons, soot, dust, smoke particles, and acids from aerosols that are smaller than 10 microns in diameter. RSPM constitutes 55% of SPM.

### Sulfur Dioxide ($SO_2$)

*Sulfur dioxide* is produced by the burning of fossil fuels and by some industrial processes such as smelting of metals, etc.

## Health Hazards

Air provides us with oxygen, which is essential for all life forms. Air pollution can cause problems for humans, animals, and plants. Major health hazards in humans include respiratory illness, heart disease, anemia, and nervous system disorders.

The following table shows various air pollutants and their associated health hazards.

| Pollutant | Adverse Health Effects |
|-----------|------------------------|
| RSPM | Respiratory illness, including chronic bronchitis and asthma; heart disease |
| $SO_2$ | Heart disease, respiratory problems, cancer, burning eyes, headache |
| $NO_2$ | Lung problems, viral infections, airway resistance, chest tightness |
| SPM | Lung disease, asthma, cancer |
| Benzene | Immune system disorders; increased risk of cancer, asthma, anemia, unconsciousness |
| Ozone | Impaired lung function, chest pain, coughing, irritation of eyes and nose |
| CO | CO poisoning can cause cherry-red lips, unconsciousness, and death by asphyxiation |
| Lead | Decreased hemoglobin synthesis, anemia, damage to the nervous and renal (kidney) systems |

## Ways to Reduce Air Pollution

- Walk or use your bicycle whenever possible.
- Use public forms of transportation.
- Form a carpool.
- Use only unleaded gasoline.
- Reduce the use of aerosols in your household.
- Plant trees and care for the trees in your neighborhood.
- Switch off all electrical appliances when not in use.
- Don't burn garden waste; compost it.

## Smog

*Smog* is haze created when air pollutants react in sunlight and combine with water vapor and dust. Smog is usually seen in winter when low wind speeds cause smoke and fog to stagnate. The prime components of smog are ground- level ozone, nitrogen oxides (NOx), volatile organic compounds (VOCs), sulfur dioxide, acidic aerosols and gases, and particulate matter.

## Acid Rain

Rainwater is acidified when emissions of sulfur dioxide and nitrogen oxides react in the atmosphere with water, oxygen, and oxidants. *Acid rain* damages plants, poisons the soil, and harms animals, fish, and other wildlife.

## Indoor Air Pollution

Smoking, cooking, heating appliances, vapors from building materials, and paints are some of the primary sources of indoor air pollution.

## Sources of Air Pollution

- Power plants, manufacturing facilities, and municipal waste incinerators
- Motor vehicles, aircraft, and marine vessels such as container ships or cruise ships
- Burning wood, fireplaces, stoves, furnaces, and incinerators
- Chemicals, dust, and burning crop waste
- Fumes from paint, varnish, aerosol sprays, and solvents
- Waste deposits in landfills
- Nuclear power plants and nuclear weapons

### Did you know?

Americans have reduced air pollutants by more than 50 million tons since 1970.

# Driving

Automobiles contribute greatly to air pollution. Most automobiles use gasoline as fuel. The burning of ordinary gasoline gives off three main pollutants: hydrocarbons, carbon monoxide, and nitrogen oxides. These pollutants increase the greenhouse effect, cause smog, contribute to ground-level ozone, and increase health hazards such as cancer and lung diseases. In the United States, cars and light trucks account for 40% of gasoline consumption and emit 20% of the country's greenhouse carbon dioxide.

## Alternative-Fuel Vehicles

*Alternative-fuel vehicles* run on fuels that are not made from petroleum. Commonly used alternative fuels include ethanol, methanol, compressed natural gas (CNG), electricity, hydrogen, liquefied petroleum gas (LPG), and biodiesel

## Alternative Fuels

| Fuel | Source/type |
|------|-------------|
| Ethanol | Produced from corn and other crops |
| Biodiesel | Produced by combining vegetable oils or animal fats with alcohol |
| Natural gas | Fossil fuel |
| Liquefied petroleum gas (LPG) | Fossil fuel |
| Hydrogen | Produced by nuclear power, burning fossil fuels, or renewable resources, such as hydropower |

## Hybrid-Electric Vehicles

*Hybrid-electric vehicles* are powered by both an internal combustion engine and an electric motor. Hybrid cars reduce fuel consumption and tailpipe emissions, thereby reducing pollution.

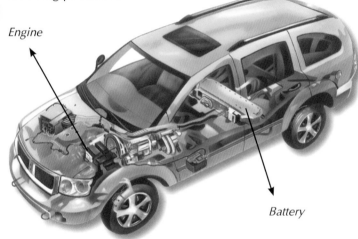

*Engine*

*Battery*

## Electric Vehicles

*Electric vehicles* are powered by electric motors and rechargeable batteries. They are energy-efficient and environment-friendly. Electric vehicles do not emit tailpipe pollution.

## Tips for Green Driving

All drivers can contribute to reducing air pollution by changing their driving habits:

- Avoid driving at high speed.
- Buy a fuel-efficient vehicle.
- Do not overfill your gasoline tank.
- Try to refuel after dark.
- Buy vehicles that emit less pollution.
- Use alternative-fuel vehicles such as electric vehicles.
- Avoid idling for long periods.
- Keep your car well-maintained, especially the emissions-control system.
- Keep tires properly inflated.
- Maintain your vehicle's air-conditioning system—check regularly for leakages.

## Top Five Global-Warming Polluters

1. United States
2. China
3. Russia
4. Japan
5. United Kingdom

### Did you know?

One gallon of burned gasoline pumps 28 pounds of carbon dioxide into the atmosphere. An average car emits about 63 tons of carbon dioxide over its lifetime.

# Public Transportation

Public transportation is a system usually provided by the government to get people from one place to another. Public transportation systems generally include buses, subways, cable cars, monorails, and ferry boats. Using public transportation is more environment-friendly and less carbon-intensive than traveling in private vehicles. It can help reduce carbon dioxide emissions and save millions of gallons of gasoline. In 2005, public transportation reduced carbon dioxide emissions by 6.9 million metric tons.

## Benefits of Public Transportation

- Conserves energy by reducing the amount of fossil fuel burned. Every year American households save more than $1,399 worth of gasoline.
- Reduces emission of harmful gases such as carbon monoxide by 95% and carbon dioxide and nitrogen oxides by 50% per passenger mile as compared to private vehicles and thus improves air quality.
- Generates jobs and helps the economy. An investment of one dollar in a public transportation project gives four to nine dollars in return.

- Decreases commuting costs and saves money in comparison to individual commuting.
- Provides safe and stress-free journeys.
- Reduces traffic congestion and saves time. Every year the American government saves $18 billion by reducing congestion costs.
- Provides choices according to individual requirements; for instance, paratransit services are provided to senior citizens and people with disabilities.

## Air Transportation

Air transportation connects various destinations around the world. It is considered the fastest mode of transportation and is often preferred in long-distance commuting.

Aircraft release harmful gases and particles that contribute to 3.5% of the forces responsible for global change. An aircraft engine releases around 70% $CO_2$, 30% $H_2O$, and less than 1% of other gases and particles.

## Heavy Rail Transit

*Heavy rail* (also known as metro, subway, rapid transit, or rapid rail) is an electrified, high-speed train that can carry around 10,000 passengers per hour. Successfully operating heavy rail transit systems include the San Francisco BART, the Chicago "L," the New York City subway, the Washington D.C. Metro, the London Underground, the Delhi Metro, and the Hong Kong MTR.

### Did you know?

Each year, using public transportation saves nearly 1.4 billion gallons of gas in the United States, which is equivalent to saving almost 4 million gallons of gas every day.

## Light Rail

*Light rail* (also known as streetcar, tramway, or trolley) is similar to heavy rail transit. It is, however, used for shorter distances and can carry fewer passengers. Successfully operating light-rail transit systems include the San Francisco Muni Metro, the Boston MBTA Green Line, the Stadtbahn in Germany, and the Hong Kong KCR Light Rail.

## Trolleybus

*Trolleybuses* (also called trackless buses or trackless trams) are electric buses that are powered by overhead wires. Many cities around the world have trolley buses. Seattle and Vancouver are two cities where trolleybuses are operating successfully.

## Bus

*Buses* are the most common means of public transit. However, they are not environment-friendly, as they run on gasoline or diesel, which contributes to air pollution. To reduce pollution and make buses environment-friendly, many countries have introduced hybrid buses and buses that run on alternative fuels like compressed natural gas (CNG) and biodiesel.

# Permafrost

Permafrost is a permanently frozen layer of soil. Permafrost occurs at higher altitudes, and its thickness varies from less than three feet to more than 3,000 feet. Permafrost is made up of soil, sediment, or rock that has been below 32° F for at least two years. Permafrost preserves organic materials and restricts water movement and plant growth. It covers nearly 25% of Earth's land surface. About 99% of Greenland, 80% of Alaska, 50% of Russia, 40% to 50% of Canada, and 20% of China has permafrost.

## Global Warming and Permafrost

Not all greenhouse gases are released by human activities. Permafrost contains large amounts of carbon-rich grass and animal bones that have been trapped inside for thousands of years. Global warming could thaw or melt this permafrost, resulting in the release of carbon into the atmosphere as a greenhouse gas. Thawing of the permafrost could release about 100 gigatons of carbon. One gigaton is equal to one billion tons.

## Permafrost Zones

### Continuous Permafrost Zone

The *continuous permafrost zone* is an unbroken layer of frozen soil that occurs in the Arctic region. Greenland lies within this zone.

### Discontinuous Permafrost Zone

The *discontinuous permafrost zone* is an irregular zone that exists as scattered pockets of unfrozen ground. It occurs where annual mean surface temperature is between 23° F and 32° F. Alaska lies within this zone. The discontinuous permafrost zone is divided into two subzones: the *widespread permafrost zone* and the *sporadic permafrost zone*.

## Thawing Permafrost in the Arctic

The Arctic region has large zones of permafrost. This region stores about 14% of the carbon found in Earth's soil. Thawing of the permafrost would release carbon, increasing global warming. The Arctic region also has about 450 billion tons of methane gas trapped within its permafrost zone. If the permafrost melts, this methane will be released into the atmosphere.

## Thawing Permafrost in Alaska

About 85% of Alaska is permafrost. Global warming has led to thawing of the permafrost, which has led to depletion of water resources and vegetation as well as soil erosion. Thawing permafrost creates shallow pits

and depressions that damage vegetation and also adversely affects agriculture. It causes soil erosion as well as sedimentation and siltation in rivers.

## Adverse Effects of Melting Permafrost

- Loss of soil quality due to erosion
- Decrease in soil moisture, which affects agriculture
- Release of carbon and methane, which will increase global warming
- Unstable ground for buildings and roads
- Damaging of oil pipelines, homes, and other buildings
- Changes in soil, landscape, agriculture, and atmosphere would lead to climate change, bringing about corresponding socioeconomic change in a region

### Did you know?

Almost one-half of the world's permafrost is in Russia and Siberia, and one-third is in Canada.

# Green Homes

Green homes are eco-friendly buildings. These houses are referred to as "green" because they are sustainable and use fewer resources. Green homes consume less energy and water. They are made from eco-friendly materials that do not harm the environment. They also protect human health and provide a better place to live and work. Green homes improve indoor air quality and utilize renewable resources such as sunlight, rainwater, and biomass.

## Why do we build green homes?

Homes and buildings also contribute to global warming. In the United States, they account for 38% of the emissions of carbon dioxide, which is a powerful greenhouse gas. Green homes help the environment as well as the economy of any place. They reduce operating costs and increase environmental performance. Energy efficiency measures used in green homes lower electricity, water, and gas bills. Green homes minimize waste and use recycle materials during their construction. The houses are well-insulated and have good ventilation systems and moisture barriers.

## Energy Star

Energy Star is a U.S. government program that certifies and labels products that are energy efficient for use in homes. Energy Star helps to reduce high energy bills and improve comfort in homes by rating the efficiency of appliances such as air conditioners, fans, refrigerators, and computers. In the United States, almost 750,000 homes are Energy Star qualified. These homes have saved up to a billion kilowatt hours of electricity and 100 million therms (about 250,000 tons of oil equivalents) of natural gas. These homes have also reduced the amount of greenhouse gases released into the atmosphere.

### Did you know?

In the United States, buildings account for 39% of total energy use, 12% of water consumption, and 68% of electricity consumption.

## Improving Energy Efficiency at Home

### Plug Air Leakages

Sealing all gaps and reducing air leakage into homes can reduce heating and cooling by almost 30%.

### Conserve Water

Using simple water-conservation devices such as low-flow showerheads and tank insulation jackets, and replacing old and leaking plumbing fixtures, can save hundreds of dollars on your utility bills.

### Use Energy-Efficient Windows

Energy-efficient windows can reduce heating and cooling by increasing surface temperature. They also protect the house and reduce mold growth by decreasing condensation.

### Use Energy-Efficient Light Bulbs

Energy-efficient light bulbs last longer and save on electric bills. They also help to keep the home cooler by reducing waste heat.

### Use Energy-Efficient Appliances

Homes with poor insulation and older electrical appliances are major contributors to global warming. Using energy-efficient refrigerators, washing machines, dryers, and dishwashers helps save both water and energy and reduces energy bills.

## Other Methods and Ways

Green roofs, rain gardens, and using packed gravel for parking lots instead of concrete or asphalt all help keep our homes cool and replenish groundwater.

# Collaborative Housing

Collaborative housing, or cohousing, is a type of housing community. It is a planned community that combines the privacy of individual homes with the advantages of living in a community. Residents, often known as cohousers, plan, design, and maintain the community themselves. Cohousing has self-contained private residences. They also share common facilities such as a community dining and sitting room, children's playrooms, workshops, guest rooms, and laundry.

## Cohousing Saves Valuable Resources

The idea behind cohousing is to save resources by living in a community and working together. Most cohousing communities are environment-friendly. Cohousing saves heating and maintenance costs. It also reduces the amount of energy used for various purposes. The idea of cohousing originated in Denmark in the 1960s. Later, in the early 1980s, architects Kathryn McCamant and Charles Durrett promoted cohousing in the United States. Cohousing communities in North America range in size from 9 to 44 households.

## Characteristics of Collaborative Housing

**All-around participation:** A cohousing community is planned, designed, and maintained by cohousers themselves. Usually, cohousers participate in all the processes of building and living in the community. This helps them to meet all their basic and long-term needs.

**Community design:** The architecture and layout of the buildings is designed to create a sense of community among cohousers. Typically, all houses face each other across a pathway or courtyard. A common house, built in a central location, serves as a community center. Cars are parked on the periphery to keep the residential area pollution- and car-free.

**Community facilities:** Cohousing communities have a common house for communal facilities and activities. The common facilities include a dining area, sitting area, common kitchen, play area, library, laundry, exercise room, lawns and gardens, and guest rooms.

**Managing the community:** A cohousing community is managed and developed by the cohousers themselves. Cohousers meet regularly to solve the problems of the community. The residents develop different programs and policies for the community. Cohousers also share all work within the community.

**Decisions by consensus:** A cohousing community has leaders, but no one person dominates the community. Everyone is given a role according to his or her abilities or interests. All decisions are made by consensus, and voting policies also exist in some cohousing communities.

**Source of income:** A cohousing community is not responsible for the income of its cohousers. The members of the community have to work for their finances and income. The community does not pay its residents for the maintenance work of the community.

### Did you know?

A *kibbutz* is a collective community in Israel. The first kibbutz was built on the bank of the Jordan River in 1909.

## Cohousing and the Environment

Cohousing communities provide an opportunity to reduce, reuse, and recycle. They also help create a healthy social environment. Cohousing helps reduce energy consumption by making common meals and using a common laundry, thus saving on energy. The comfortably sized homes in cohousing communities save construction and maintenance costs. Cohousing communities have open green space for recreation and conservation. There are community gardens in which people grow vegetables to be used in community meals. People follow the sharing policy, which means less consumption of nonrenewable resources. Residents share automobiles for trips to the market and other destinations.

## Benefits of Cohousing

- Ideal balance between privacy and community
- Social interaction and support
- Lower living cost
- Savings on meals
- Healthy lifestyle
- Reasonably priced homes
- Social security by living in community
- Safe environment
- Better childcare
- Caring neighbors
- Sharing of resources

## Cohousing Communities Around the World

Cohousing communities originated in Denmark and have now spread around the world. Many countries, including the United States, Canada, Australia, Sweden, New Zealand, the Netherlands, Germany, France, Belgium, and Austria, now have cohousing communities.

# Deforestation and Altering the Carbon Balance

Forests cover about a third of Earth's total land area. Forests are an important ecosystem and crucial for all life on Earth. They help to reduce the rate of global warming by absorbing carbon dioxide from the air. Human activity, pollution, and acid rain are slowly destroying forests. Human activities like logging and burning of trees have caused large-scale destruction of forests. Most of this deforestation takes place to provide land for agricultural, residential, or industrial purposes.

## Carbon Reservoir

Forests are the most efficient ecosystem on Earth. They absorb carbon dioxide from the atmosphere and store it as carbon in wood, vegetation, and soil. Most of the carbon dioxide in the atmosphere is a result of the burning of fossil fuels and other human activities. Earth's forests act as a reservoir or sink for the carbon dioxide. Forests store about one trillion tons of carbon, which is twice the amount found in the atmosphere. Deforestation diminishes this reservoir of carbon dioxide.

## Forests and Greenhouse Gases

Deforestation releases enormous amounts of carbon dioxide, a greenhouse gas, into the atmosphere. About 17% of the world's atmospheric carbon dioxide comes from deforestation. Each year, deforestation adds almost 6 billion tons of carbon dioxide into the atmosphere. This is almost the same amount of carbon dioxide produced by the United States.

## Earth's Forest Cover

Most of Earth's forests have disappeared. It is estimated that more than 80% of Earth's natural forests have already been destroyed. Since 1900, most of West Africa's coastal rainforests have disappeared. Now only 10% of the rainforests remain. Earth's two largest surviving rainforests, in Brazil and Indonesia, are disappearing at an alarming rate, mostly because of human activities. Logging, land clearing, and forest fires are responsible for this depleting forest cover.

## How Deforestation Happens

Deforestation is brought about by the following:
- Cutting forests and woodlands for agricultural land
- Clearing forests for commercial development
- Development of cash crops
- Cattle ranching
- Commercial logging
- Clearing forests for agriculture
- Felling trees for firewood
- Felling trees for building material
- Cattle grazing

## What can we do?
- Plant new trees to remove carbon from the air.
- Replant trees in deforested areas.
- Plant trees in non-forested lands.
- Limit activities like logging and overgrazing.
- Buy recycled products.
- Create public awareness.
- Create green areas around our homes and community.

## Forests and Rainfall

Forests absorb large amounts of sunlight. They absorb almost 90% of all the sunlight striking Earth, and only about a tenth is reflected. The energy absorbed by forests helps to stimulate *convection currents* in the air. Convection currents are caused by the rising and falling of hot air. These convection currents help to increase the amount of rainfall in forests. Typically, forests in tropical areas are very wet and humid because they receive a lot of rainfall. On the other hand, deforested areas absorb about 80% of the sunlight. Deforested areas, therefore, become drier with time and may turn arid. As the area of deforestation increases, so does its impact on the climate.

## Forests and Life

Forests use sunlight for photosynthesis. *Photosynthesis* is the process by which plants convert carbon dioxide and water into carbohydrates using sunlight. Photosynthesis releases oxygen as a waste product, which is vital for all life on Earth. This also helps to regulate the natural greenhouse effect.

## Effects of Deforestation
- Destruction of unique environments
- Loss of precious medicinal plants
- No recycling of water
- Greenhouse gas emissions
- Desertification
- Frequent dust storms
- Animals and plants face extinction.
- Soil becomes dry and cracked because of exposure to the sun.
- Loss of shaded area leads to increase in temperature extremes.
- It is hard for rain to soak into the soil, so flooding may occur.
- Nutrients from soil are washed out by the rain.

### Did you know?

Forests are home to about 70% of all land animals and plants.

# Fossil Fuels

Fossil fuels are energy resources found in Earth's crust. They formed many hundreds of millions of years ago from the remains of long-buried plants and other organisms. Coal, oil, and natural gas are the three major forms of fossil fuels. They are nonrenewable energy sources because they take hundreds of millions of years to create. Fossil fuels provide most of the energy used to generate electricity, heat, and cooling for our homes and power our motor vehicles and airplanes. The demand for fossil fuel has increased with a growing world population. The burning of fossil fuels releases carbon dioxide, a greenhouse gas. The large-scale burning of fossil fuels increases global warming and causes acid rain.

## Where is fossil fuel used?

- Fossil fuels supply over 85% of the world's commercial energy.
- Fossil fuels supply 65% of the world's electricity.
- Fossil fuels provide 97% of the energy for transportation.

## Benefits of Fossil Fuels

Fossil fuels are an important source of energy. They are useful as fuel because of their low cost and easy availability. Fossil fuels such as coal, oil, and natural gas are found abundantly on Earth. Fossil fuels can easily be mined and drilled at a low cost. Coal is the most abundant fossil fuel and is found worldwide.

## Coal

*Coal* is a hard, rocklike substance that formed from the remains of decaying plants. It is an impure form of carbon and an abundant fossil resource. Coal is recovered from Earth by mining. There are three main types of coal: anthracite, bituminous, and lignite. Each type contains different amounts of carbon. Anthracite contains 95% carbon and is the hardest and most expensive coal. Bituminous coal contains 70% carbon. Lignite is the softest and contains less than 50% carbon. Coal is used as a basic energy source in industries and homes. About 50% of the electricity generated in the United States comes from coal.

## Petroleum

Petroleum, or oil, is a naturally occurring liquid. Petroleum is refined to make fuels and lubricants. One barrel of crude oil gives 19.5 gallons of gasoline, 9.2 gallons of distilled fuel oil, 401 gallons of jet fuel, and 1.9 gallons of liquefied gases. The Middle East has more than half of the world's known oil reserves. The other petroleum products derived from crude oil are petrochemical ingredients like plastics, inks, tires, and pharmaceutical products.

### Did you know?

Coal is a relatively cheap fuel that can provide energy at $1 to $2 per million Btu as compared to $6 to $12 per million Btu for oil and natural gas.

## Natural Gas

*Natural gas* is another form of natural fossil fuel. It is lighter than air and highly flammable. It is found as a mixture of hydrocarbon and non-hydrocarbon gases under porous rock forms. The main component in natural gas is methane, a chemical compound made of carbon and hydrogen atoms. In comparison to fossil fuel, natural gas emits fewer harmful chemicals. It is used for cooking in homes as well as for running turbines to produce electricity. Natural gas can be compressed and used in many forms. Compressed natural gas, or CNG, reduces the emission of greenhouse gases to a large extent. Natural gas reserves can be found in Russia, Iran, Qatar, Saudi Arabia, United Arab Emirates, and the United States.

## Uses of Fossil Fuels

1. **Providing electricity**: Fossil fuels help to generate electricity. Coal is the most important electricity generation source, making up more than half of all resources. Natural gas and petroleum are also used in electricity generation.
2. **Fueling transportation**: Fossil fuels are also used as fuel in automobiles and other forms of transportation. Petroleum-based fuels are standard fuels used in vehicles. The transportation infrastructure of pipelines and gas stations is built around petroleum-based fuels.
3. **Heating and cooling**: Fossil fuels such as natural gas and oil are used in heating and cooling. People in cold countries spend the cold and harsh winters by heating their homes and offices with these fuels. Air conditioners used in hot places consume electricity generated from fossil fuels.

# Ocean Acidification

Oceans are large bodies of water on Earth. They cover more than 70% of Earth's surface and contain about 97% of all water on our planet. Oceans play a major role in Earth's carbon cycle. They absorb a large amount of carbon dioxide from the atmosphere. An increase in the amount of carbon dioxide in the atmosphere has resulted in more carbon dioxide being absorbed by the oceans. Carbon dioxide dissolved in the ocean reacts with water to form carbonic acid. This results in *ocean acidification*.

## Ocean Water and the pH Scale

Oceans have slightly alkaline properties rather than acidic properties. The pH scale determines the acidic or alkaline properties of any substance. The pH level 7 is neutral; higher than 7 is alkaline and lower than 7 is acidic. The historical global mean value of seawater is about 8.16, which makes it slightly alkaline.

### What makes oceans acidic?

In the atmosphere, carbon dioxide is released in large amounts by burning of fossil fuels. About half of this carbon dioxide is absorbed by oceans. It is estimated that the oceans have absorbed too much carbon dioxide. This has led to a decrease in the pH of Earth's oceans. Biosystems like oceans are adapted to a narrow range of pH. Even a small change in pH may lead to large changes in ocean chemistry and ecosystem functioning. The oceans' surface pH will soon reach its lowest level in 300 million years. Therefore, the increased atmospheric $CO_2$ is a serious problem that needs to be tackled immediately.

## Effects on Marine Life

The carbon dioxide dissolved in seawater increases the acidity of water. *Acidity* is the amount of hydrogen ion concentration in the water. The higher the hydrogen ion concentration, the more acidic the water will be. These hydrogen ions in turn combine with the carbonate ions and form bicarbonate. The formation of bicarbonate ions removes carbonate ions from the water, which then cannot be used by the marine organisms to form their shells.

## Adverse Effects of Ocean Acidification

- Rising acidity of seawater lowers the carbonate ions in the water, making it difficult or impossible for corals and shelled organisms to form their shells.
- In the Antarctic Ocean, tiny shelled plankton, which are the major food source of whales, fish, and other animals, suffer first.
- The high levels of carbon dioxide make it difficult for fish and shellfish to breathe and reproduce underwater.
- Chemical changes in seawater reduce the oceans' ability to absorb carbon dioxide from the atmosphere and thus speed up the rate of global warming.

### What can be done?

We can take certain steps in the next five to ten years to lessen ocean acidification:

- Keep regular records of the calcification of pteropods, corals, and other shelled organisms.
- Study the potential consequences of sudden drops in the number of shelled organisms.
- Determine the effects of seasonal warming and cooling on acidification.

### Did you know?

By the year 2100, the pH level of ocean water may fall by 0.4 units, which means a 150% increase in ocean acidification.

# Population Shifts of Plants and Animals

Global warming is continually making the planet warmer. Plant and animal populations are being affected by global warming. It is estimated that in the next 50 years, more than a million plant and animal species will move toward extinction due to global warming.

## Earlier Than Usual

According to scientists, flowers are blooming earlier, birds are laying eggs earlier, and mammals are ending their hibernation periods earlier now than in the past. These events are occurring, on average, 5.1 days earlier for every decade. For example, in the United States, field biologists kept track of 21,000 tree swallow nests over the last 40 years. They found that female swallows lay eggs nine days earlier now than their average egg-laying date 40 years ago.

## Plants and Animals Facing Extinction

Recent scientific studies have revealed that increases in global average temperatures may have adverse effects on the living world. Scientists believe that if the global average temperature increases by more than 2.7° F to 4.5° F, then about 20% to 30% of plant and animal species are at risk of extinction. In 2003, more than 12,000 species (out of 40,000 assessed) were at risk of extinction. One in eight bird species, 13% of the world's flowering plants, and 25% of all mammals were at risk.

## Moving Species

Scientists have discovered that about 2,000 species of plants and animals are moving toward the poles. Every 10 years they are moving, on average, about 3.8 miles. Similarly, in alpine areas, plant and animal species have been moving up in elevation at a rate of about 18 feet higher every 10 years during the second half of the 20th century.

## Changes We Can See

- Marmots spend the winter hibernating. Now they end their hibernation period about three weeks earlier in comparison to 30 years ago.
- Polar bears are getting thinner and weaker compared to the polar bears of 20 years earlier.
- Several species of fish are moving northward in search of cooler waters.
- A gene found in fruit flies living in hot, dry conditions has spread to cooler regions.

### Did you know?

If global average temperatures increase by more than 2.7° F to 4.5° F, about 20% to 30% of all plant and animal species are likely to become extinct.

## Global Warming and Plant Shifts

- Spring wildflowers on the Hudson highlands of southeastern New York are found to be blooming 19.8 days earlier, on average, than they did 50 years ago in six of the 15 species.
- In Wisconsin, flowering plants such as wild geraniums, columbine, and other species are also blooming earlier than before.
- In the Olympic Mountains in Washington state, the trees of the sub-alpine forest have gradually shifted to higher-elevation alpine meadows. Mangrove forests are also being lost in Bermuda and other places.
- The algae growing underneath the shrinking sea ice in the Antarctic Peninsula region has diminished due to increasing temperatures.

## Global Warming and Animal Population Shifts

- In the past 30 years, dozens of frog species have come to the edge of extinction due to rising temperatures.
- Polar bears have to swim longer distances to reach ice floes, and sometimes it's too far and they drown. It is predicted by the U.S. Geological Survey that by the mid-21st century two-thirds of the world's polar bear subpopulations will become extinct due to melting of the Arctic ice cap.
- Warmer ocean and air temperatures are resulting in the shift of shoreline sea life toward the north.
- The population of penguins has also decreased by 33% in parts of Antarctica in the past 25 years due to declines in winter sea-ice habitat.

# Fire

Fire is a chemical reaction. The chemical reaction in fire produces heat and light, which we call *flame*. Three things are necessary to create fire: oxygen, fuel, and heat. Fire gathers oxygen and heat from the air. Hotter temperatures on Earth mean hotter and drier summers. Hot weather dehydrates the forest floor, which creates the perfect conditions for fire. The dryness of the weather also prevents rain from dampening fires. Large fires release tons of carbon dioxide into the atmosphere. This causes more global warming.

# Wildfire

*Wildfires* are unplanned and uncontrolled fires. These large, devastating fires destroy agricultural fields, trees, and houses, and often kill animals and sometimes people. Wildfires occur around the world, including the forest areas of Australia, the United States, and Canada. The prevalent times of wildfires are summer and fall and during droughts.

## Drought and Wildfire

Warmer temperatures lead to *drought* conditions. The evaporation rate increases during summer and fall. This worsens the drought conditions and creates ideal conditions for wildfires. In 2006, some 100,000 wildfires were reported. Around 10 million acres of land was burned, which was 125% above the 10-year average.

## Types of Wildfires

- Surface wildfires are the most common fires. They burn along the forest floor, moving at a slow pace. Surface wildfires burn and damage fallen trees, grasses, and shrubs.
- Ground wildfires occur easily. They usually start by lightning and burn below the forest floor slowly. Ground fires burn tree roots, dead wood, and dry leaves.

- Crown fires are the most dangerous wildfires. They are spread by rapid winds and burn the tops of the trees.

## Health Hazards of Wildfire

- Burns
- Respiratory complications
- Inhalation injuries
- Cardiovascular problems

The following table shows the total number of wildfires in the United States and the number of acres they burned.

| Totals as of Dec. 28, 2007 | Number of Fires | Number of Acres Burned |
|---|---|---|
| 2007 | 85,583 | 9,318,710 |
| 2006 | 96,326 | 9,871,863 |
| 2005 | 66,020 | 8,681,252 |
| 2004 | 65,878 | 8,094,531 |
| 2003 | 63,269 | 3,959,223 |
| 2002 | 73,423 | 7,182,979 |
| 2001 | 83,996 | 3,570,225 |
| 2000 | 92,250 | 7,393,493 |
| 5-Year Average (2003-2007) | 75,415 | 7,985,116 |
| 10-Year Average (1997-2006) | 78,482 | 7,904,524 |

## Ways to Prevent Fires

- Make fires away from trees or bushes. The blowing ash and cinders may cause wildfires.
- Be ready to extinguish the fire quickly and completely.
- Never leave a fire burning, even a burning cigarette. Immediately put it out; otherwise it could start a wildfire.

### Did you know?

In 1997, peatlands in Southeast Asia burned and released about 2.67 billion tons of carbon dioxide. This was equivalent to 40% of a year's global fossil fuel combustion.

# CFLs

The *compact fluorescent lamp*, or CFL, is a modern light bulb that is an efficient alternative to incandescent bulbs. It radiates a different kind of light than that of incandescent bulbs. The main component of CFLs is phosphorus, which gives off a soft, white light. These bulbs are 75% more energy efficient and last 10 times longer than incandescent bulbs. CFLs also cut carbon dioxide emission to 125 billion pounds annually. They save energy and reduce greenhouse gas emissions.

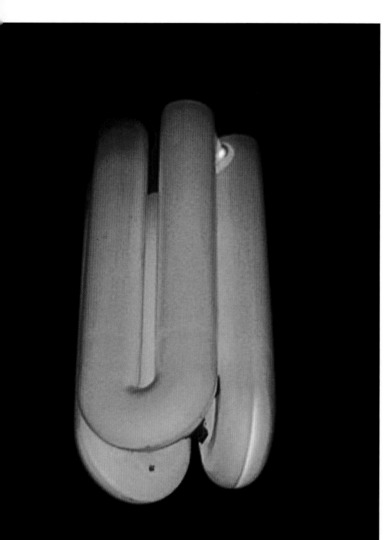

### CFLs and Global Warming

Global warming can be reduced by using energy-saving bulbs. CFLs consume up to 75% less energy than incandescent light bulbs. They reduce the emissions of carbon dioxide, sulfur oxide, and high-level nuclear waste by saving electricity.

### CFLs Contain Harmful Mercury

*Mercury* is a chemical found naturally in the environment. This heavy metal is an essential component of CFLs. CFLs contain a small amount of mercury. Mercury is a neurotoxin that is poisonous to humans, just like lead. Mercury may be harmful, but CFLs are beneficial for the environment. Many environmental groups want manufacturers to limit the amount of mercury content in CFLs. They also want the proper disposal of CFLs so that the mercury from them does not pose a health hazard.

## Advantages of CFLs

- Saves energy
- Saves about $25 to $45 over the life of the bulb
- Reduces emission of greenhouse gases
- Reduces water and air pollution
- Lasts up to 10 times longer than incandescent bulbs
- Gives warm, soft-white, high-quality light
- Is flexible and can be used anywhere
- Different ranges in wattages, size, and shape
- Safer than halogen bulbs
- Produces 90% less heat

## Disadvantages of CFLs

- Emits a small amount of ultraviolet rays
- Contains toxic mercury, which requires proper disposal
- Doesn't work properly in cold temperatures
- Switching on and off frequently reduces the life of CFLs
- More expensive than incandescent bulbs
- Not available in all stores
- Produces low light
- Larger than regular incandescent bulbs; may not fit in some fixtures

## How to Clean Up a Broken Compact Fluorescent Bulb

- Keep windows open to let the harmful mercury vapors go out.
- Vacate the room for at least 15 minutes or more.
- Do not use your bare hands; use disposable rubber gloves.
- Scoop up the broken parts and powder with stiff paper or cardboard.
- Use wet wipers to clean the area.
- Seal the wastes in a plastic bag before disposing of it.
- Never use a vacuum cleaner or broom for cleaning up.
- Safely put the bag in your trash container for safe disposal.
- Always wash your hands properly after the disposal.

### Did you know?

The United States could save enough electricity to close 21 power plants by switching over five highly used light bulbs to compact fluorescents. It would save about 800 billion kilowatt-hours.

# Indoor Air Pollution

Indoor air pollution occurs within a house, a building, or an enclosed area. Recent studies have shown that indoor air is more polluted than outdoor air. The level of indoor air pollution is often as much as two to five times higher than outdoor air pollution. Indoor air pollution is caused by mold, bacteria, allergens, and chemicals. People who spend most of their time indoors, such as infants, children, women, and the elderly, are most affected by indoor air pollution. Each year, indoor air pollution causes about 1.6 million deaths around the world.

## Sources of Indoor Air Pollution

Indoor air pollution is caused by a variety of sources. These include combustion of fuel, building materials, bioaerosols, and radon. Substances used as combustion sources, such as coal, wood, oil, kerosene, gas, and tobacco, are the major sources of indoor air pollution. Building materials include asbestos-containing products, pressed wood furniture, household cleaning and maintenance products, furnishings, and heating and cooling systems. Bioaerosols are microscopic organisms. These include molds, bacteria, viruses, pollen, dust mites, animal dander, and cat saliva. Radon is a naturally occurring radioactive gas that is a serious health hazard. Radon comes from rocks and dirt and can become trapped in houses and buildings. It can enter homes through cracks in the foundation floor and walls, drains, and other openings. It has been found that the ground below one out of every 15 homes in the United States has high levels of radon, which may increase the risk of cancer.

| Pollutants | Sources | Health Effects |
|---|---|---|
| Radon | Ground under the building | Lung cancer |
| Lead | Lead-based paint, contaminated soil | Damages kidneys and the central nervous system |
| Formaldehyde | Furniture polished with formaldehyde; plywood | Headache, nausea, skin irritation, watery eyes |
| Toluene, phenols, ketones | Paints, varnishes, air fresheners, cleansers | Eyes-nose-throat (ENT) irritation, headache |
| Carbon dioxide, carbon monoxide, and oxides of sulfur | Combustion of fuels, tobacco smoking | Fatigue, dizziness, confusion |
| Suspended particles | Tobacco smoking, combustion of solid fuels | Nasal congestion, asthma, burning sensation in eyes |
| Pesticides | Moth and mosquito repellants and insecticides | ENT irritation, cancer, kidney failure |
| Biological pollutants (bacteria, mites, molds, pollens) | Wet or moist walls, ceiling, and carpets | Allergy, shortness of breath, ENT irritation |

## Indoor Air Pollution and Human Health

Indoor air pollution is harmful to human health. Polluted indoor air can cause several serious diseases and health disorders.

## Plants That Reduce Indoor Air Pollution

- Aloe vera: removes emissions from most toxic materials
- Chinese evergreen, bamboo palm, and lily: reduce many toxic materials
- Chrysanthemum: reduces toxins such as ammonia, benzene, and formaldehyde
- English ivy: reduces petroleum-based toxins
- Fig tree: reduces formaldehyde
- Spider plant: eliminates formaldehyde

## How to Prevent Indoor Air Pollution

- Do not smoke indoors.
- Do not burn charcoal indoors.
- Install and use ventilators in your kitchen and bathroom.
- Make sure to clean exhaust fans regularly.
- Use safe cleaning products and avoid those with warning words such as "danger," "warning," or "caution."
- Clean your entire house regularly, especially the kitchen and bathroom.
- Always use high-quality plywood in furniture.
- Clean your air filters and furnace.
- Dust regularly to keep away dust mites.
- Use easy-to-clean paint and wallpaper.
- Keep indoor spaces moisture-free. Make sure to heat all rooms to avoid moisture forming on the walls and other surfaces of the unheated areas.

## Indoor Air Pollution in Developing Countries

Developing countries are the most affected by indoor air pollution. Almost 90% of rural households in developing countries depend on biomass fuel, including wood, dung, and crop residues. People burn these fuels indoors for cooking, in open fires or stoves. Wood is the most common solid fuel used for domestic purposes in developing countries. Coal is also used widely in China and South Africa. The World Health Organization estimates that more than 1.6 million deaths per year and 2.7% of the global health problems are caused by pollution created by these solid fuels.

## Adverse Health Effects of Indoor Air Pollution

- Asthma
- Cancer
- Cataracts (blindness)
- Dizziness
- Headache
- Hypertension
- Irritation in eyes, nose, and throat
- Heart diseases
- Respiratory diseases
- Tuberculosis

# Facts and Figures

1. The size of the summer polar ice cap has shrunk by more than 20% since 1979.
2. According to a U.S. Environmental Protection Agency study, rising of the global sea level by three feet by the year 2100 would submerge about 22,400 square miles of land along the Atlantic and Gulf coasts of the United States.
3. Scientists say that 69,000 square miles of Arctic ice, roughly equal to the size of Florida, has disappeared.
4. The Arctic ice cap is melting rapidly. It is expected to shrink by 40% by the year 2050 in most regions.

5. The U.S. State Department estimates that each year, clearing and erosion cause a loss of forest four times the size of Switzerland.
6. Between 1990 and 2005, Brazil has cleared over 42 million hectares of forest, which is about equal to the size of California.
7. Each year, about 20% of greenhouse gas emissions result from deforestation in developing countries.
8. During each year between 2000 and 2005, about 13 million hectares of forest in developing countries was cleared. This is nearly equal to losing more than 71,000 football fields of forest in a day.

9. About 4.4 million trees are cleared every day.
10. Each year about 1.6 billion trees are removed. Afforestation efforts replace only 0.6 billion trees, leaving a shortfall of almost 1 billion.
11. Montana's Glacier National Park now has only 27 glaciers, down from 150 in 1910.
12. A reduction of about 50% in the present global rate of deforestation could help reduce about 10% of global greenhouse gas emissions, resulting in about three billion fewer tons of carbon dioxide per year.
13. By 2100, sea level may rise between 7 and 23 inches. Rising of just 4 inches may submerge many South Sea islands and flood large parts of Southeast Asia.
14. The sun has been getting hotter over the past 60 years.
15. About 100 million people live on land that's three feet below mean sea level.
16. About 22% of the Adélie penguin population decreased during the last 25 years.

17. According to the World Bank, reduction of deforestation can deliver emission savings for less than $5 per ton of carbon dioxide.
18. Burning one gallon of gasoline puts about 28 pounds of carbon dioxide into the atmosphere.
19. An average car emits about 63 tons of carbon dioxide over its lifetime.
20. If all vehicles in the United States averaged 40 miles per gallon (mpg), that would save more than three million barrels of oil per day. This is more than the total amount of oil the United States imports from the Persian Gulf.
21. About 99% of the energy used for transcontinental flights could be reduced if people used video conferencing instead.
22. The United States could cut about 40% of its oil imports if only 1 in 10 Americans used public transportation daily.
23. Each day nearly 14 million Americans travel by public transportation.
24. By using public transportation, every American family could reduce household expenses by about $6,200 per year.

25. In the United States, about 10% of people under 18 and 7% of those aged 65 or older use public transportation; approximately 52% of public transit riders are female.
26. The industrialized countries in the northern hemisphere emit about 90% of the chlorofluorocarbons in the atmosphere.
27. Since 1950, many parts of the Arctic have warmed by 4° F to 5° F.
28. Each year, about 1.2 trillion gallons of untreated sewage, storm water, and industrial waste are added to the U.S. water supply.

# Index

# Glossary

**acid rain:** rain containing sulfur dioxide and other pollutants in dissolved form

**agriculture:** growing and raising of crops and animals for food

**algae:** small, aquatic, rootless plants such as seaweed

**altitude:** the height of an area measured from sea level

**aquatic:** ability to live or grow in or on water

**atmosphere:** the layer of gases that surround the earth

**bacteria:** microscopic, single-celled organisms that can cause diseases

**carbon dioxide:** colorless gas in the Earth's atmosphere that helps in trapping heat close to the Earth

**climate:** the usual weather of an area

**commercial:** to do with buying or selling

**component:** different parts that combine with other parts to make up a whole

**condense:** to change from a vapor or gas to a liquid

**conservation:** protection or management of a valuable resource such as water

**contaminate:** to pollute by direct contact

**continent:** one of the seven large landmasses on the earth, such as Asia or North America

**crust:** the hard, outer layer of the earth

**decompose:** to break down and decay

**deforestation:** removal of forests by cutting of trees

**depletion:** the gradual loss of non-renewable sources

**dissolve:** to separate into molecules in a liquid

**drought:** a long period of little or no rain

**ecosystem:** a complex community of living things in a physical environment

**emission:** discharge of substances into the air

**endangered:** in danger of dying out or becoming extinct

**erosion:** wearing away of land or soil by water, wind, animals, and even human activity

**evaporation:** the process by which a liquid turns to a gas

**fertilizer:** a chemical substance used to improve soil and promote plant growth

**glacier:** a large body of ice that moves very slowly

**habitat:** an environment in which a plant or animal normally lives and grows

**heat energy:** a form of energy given off by the sun or another heat source

**hemisphere:** half of the Earth on either side of the equator

**hurricane:** a severe storm with winds of 74 mph or more

**hydrogen:** a light, colorless, and odorless gas that burns well

**infrastructure:** the basic facilities required by a community, such as roads, bridges, and pipelines

**insulation:** a material designed to prevent heat from escaping

**irrigation:** the addition of water to agricultural land using sprinklers, pumps, or pipes

**molecule:** the smallest particles of an element or compound

**nutrients:** substances that help living things be healthy and grow

**organic matter:** remains of dead plants and animals

**organism:** any living structure—plant, animal, fungus, bacterium—capable of growth and reproduction

**photosynthesis:** the process through which green plants use energy from sunlight to make their own food

**plankton:** very small plants and animals that float in water and drift with ocean currents

**pollutant:** a substance that contaminates and pollutes air, water, and land

**precipitation:** falling products of condensation of water vapor in the atmosphere, as in rain, snow, or hail

**radiation:** rays or waves of energy emitted from the sun

**reservoir:** a lake that is used to store water

**resource:** something ready for use

**sediment:** small particles such as sand or gravel that settles on the land or ocean floor

**toxic:** containing poison

**ultraviolet rays:** invisible light rays emitted from the sun

**urban:** related to city or town

**vapor:** the gaseous form of something that is usually liquid

# THE LEARNING RESOURCE CENTER
## Weston Intermediate School